Michael Grejniec
ALBERT'S NAP

DO NOT
DISTURB
Albert

North-South Books

Z Z Z Z Z Z S Z Z Z Z Z Z Z Z Z

**One spring day,
Albert took a nap.**

Bzzzz...

Oh, no!

Bzzz...

Wait!

I'll get you!

Look out!

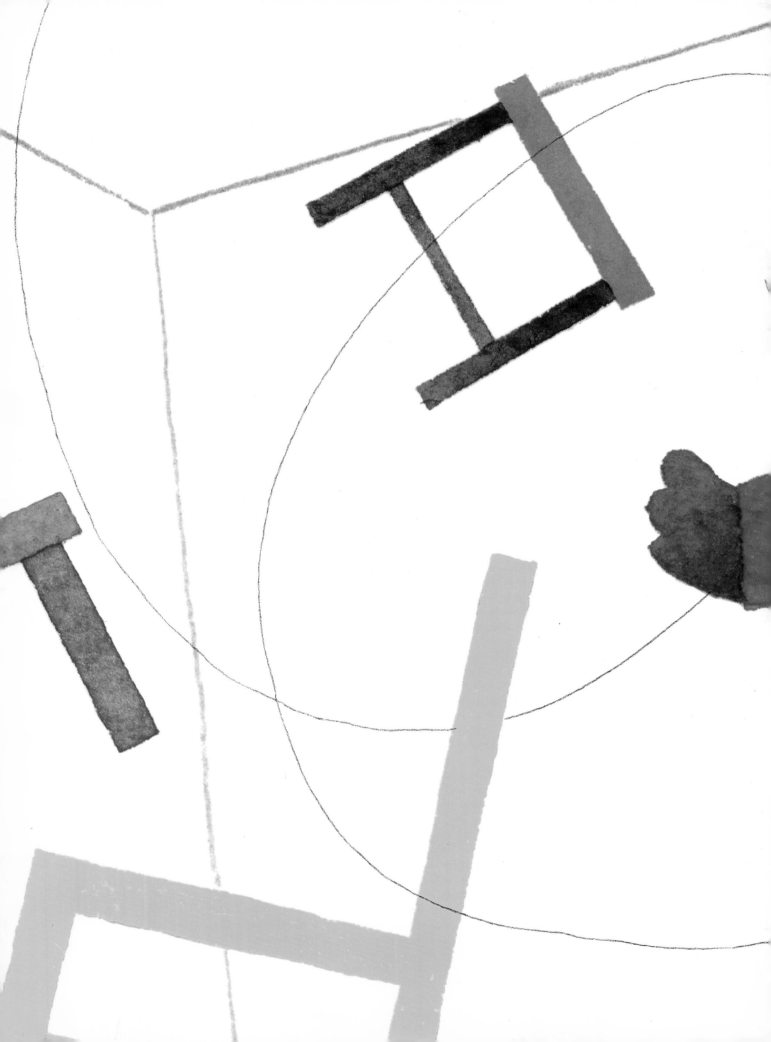

Oooops!

Bzzzzz...

Where are you?

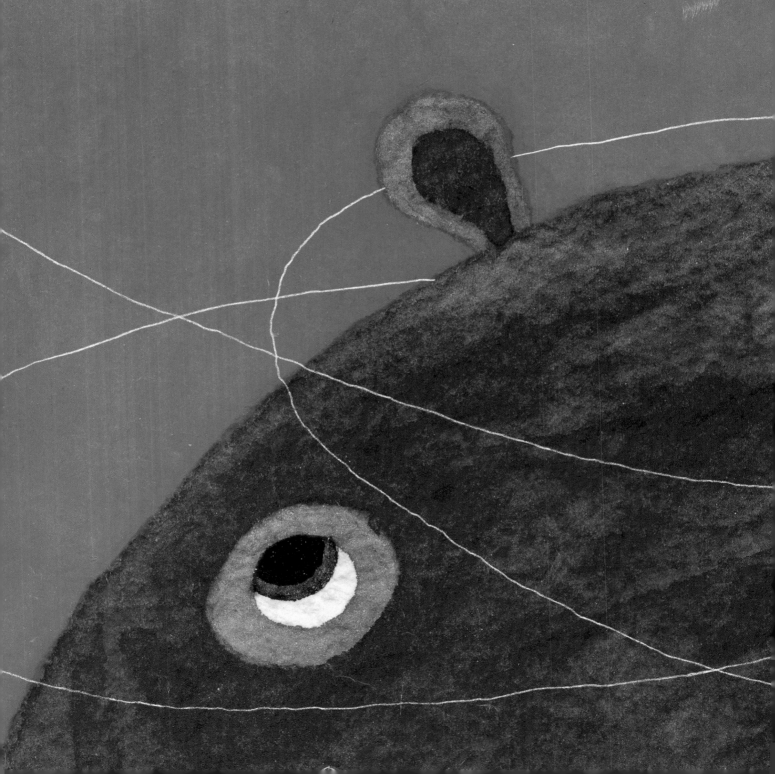

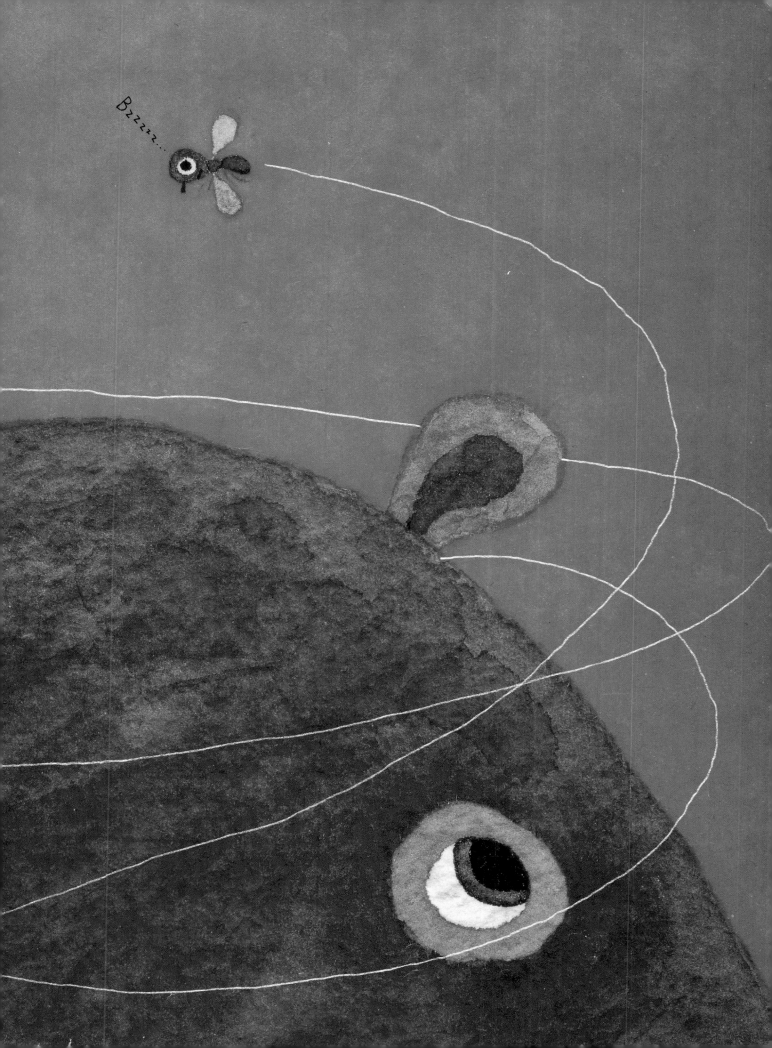

Bzzzz...

You're in trouble now!

How about this?!

Bzzzz...

Gotcha!!!

I am so tired...
I need some fresh air...

Ah, finally.

Published in the United States by North-South Books Inc., New York.
Published simultaneously in Great Britain, Canada, Australia, and New Zealand in 1995
by North-South Books, an imprint of Nord-Süd Verlag AG, Gossau Zürich, Switzerland.

Library of Congress Cataloging-in-Publication Data is available.
A CIP catalogue record for this book is available from The British Library.

The artwork was painted with watercolors, which have been greatly enlarged during the color-separation
process to accentuate both the rough surface of the watercolor paper and the rough edges
of the images. Designed and hand lettered by Michael Grejniec.

ISBN 1-55858-279-7 (trade binding)
1 3 5 7 9 TB 10 8 6 4 2
ISBN 1-55858-280-0 (library binding)
1 3 5 7 9 LB 10 8 6 4 2
Printed in Belgium

The Sesame Street Word Book

ILLUSTRATED BY TOM LEIGH

Featuring Jim Henson's Sesame Street Muppets

A GOLDEN BOOK
Published by Golden Books Publishing Company Inc.,
in cooperation with Children's Television Workshop

A Note to Parents

THE SESAME STREET WORD BOOK provides children with a rich and colorful environment in which to explore the world of words. Entertaining scenes introduce words in context to help children expand and organize their vocabulary. Detailed pictures with easy-to-read labels demonstrate that words are symbols—for actions, people, places, and things.

The variety of subjects presented also helps stimulate children's imagination. Talk with your children about the illustrations. Help them to relate the pictures to personal experience or to create imaginative stories. This book is particularly conducive to sharing between parent and child. Encourage your children to point out objects for you to identify.

The Sesame Street Word Book features your children's favorite Sesame Street friends, who open up an inviting world that you and your children will enjoy returning to again and again.

The Editors of Golden Books
and Children's Television Workshop

binoculars   camera

pigeon

Contents

Ernie and Bert at Home

Ernie and Bert live at 123 Sesame Street.
Bert is in the living room.
But where is Ernie?

curtains

window shade

clock

lamp

window

couch

chair

radio

coffee table

footstool

floor

rug

picture frame

picture

door

television

bookcase

telephone

doorknob

soapsuds

radiator

9

Ernie Takes a Bath

Ernie is in the bathtub.
He is singing to Rubber Duckie.
"Rubber Duckie, you're the one!
You make bath time lots of fun!"

shower

medicine cabinet

bathrobe

mirror

towel rack

towel

cup

Rubber
Duckie

toothbrush

soap

toothpaste

faucet

back brush

toy boat

inflatable
sea horse

bubbles

sink

peanut-butter
sandwich

bubble bath

shampoo

stool

washcloth

toilet

sponge

nailbrush

slippers

bath mat

10

oatmeal

bowls

cups

Bert's Breakfast
Can you guess what
Bert is cooking?

cabinet

glasses   plates

cookbooks

can opener

coffeepot

toaster

spice rack

teakettle

funnel

sink

stove

pan

oven

apron

potholders

dishtowel

frying pan

colander

refrigerator

measuring cup

sifter

measuring spoons

pancake turner

spatula

grater

rolling pin

spoon

cutting board

fork

knife

ladle

egg beater

11

Zoe's Room
It is raining today.
Can you guess what Zoe
is going to wear?

clock

closet

hanger

rain hat

spaceship

doll

pants

dress

blouse

mirror

raincoat

books

drawer

umbrella

party shoes

sneaker

teddy bear

truck

blue jeans

pillow

jumper

skirt

cap

sweater

lamp

bed

bedspread

toy chest

dresser

night table

toy train

rubber boots

hat

rocking chair

doll house

blocks

baseball bat

12

Getting Dressed

socks   saddle shoes

Can you put on your socks?

Can you put on
your overalls?

turtleneck

Can you pull on your shirt?

winter
cap

zipper

Can you zip up your jacket?

scarf

Can you fasten your boots?

cowgirl hat

Can you buckle your belt?

top hat

bow tie

cape

Can you put on your gloves?

cowboy hat

vest

cuff

Can you snap your snaps?

collar

night cap

pocket

Can you button your pajamas?

13

Helping Around the House

closet

mop

bucket

Ernie and Bert clean up their room.

broom

dustpan

Big Bird sweeps the steps.

pillow

bedspread

The Twiddlebugs make the bed.

glass

cup

fork

plate

knife

spoon

Grover sets the table

feather duster

Snuffy dusts the ceiling.

cloth

spray bottle

Betty Lou shines the mirror.

soapsuds

apron

rubber gloves

Cookie Monster washes the dishes.

blanket

dryer

washing machine

Oscar folds his laundry.

vacuum cleaner

BATCUUM

The Count vacuums the rug.

15

Taking Care of Baby Natasha

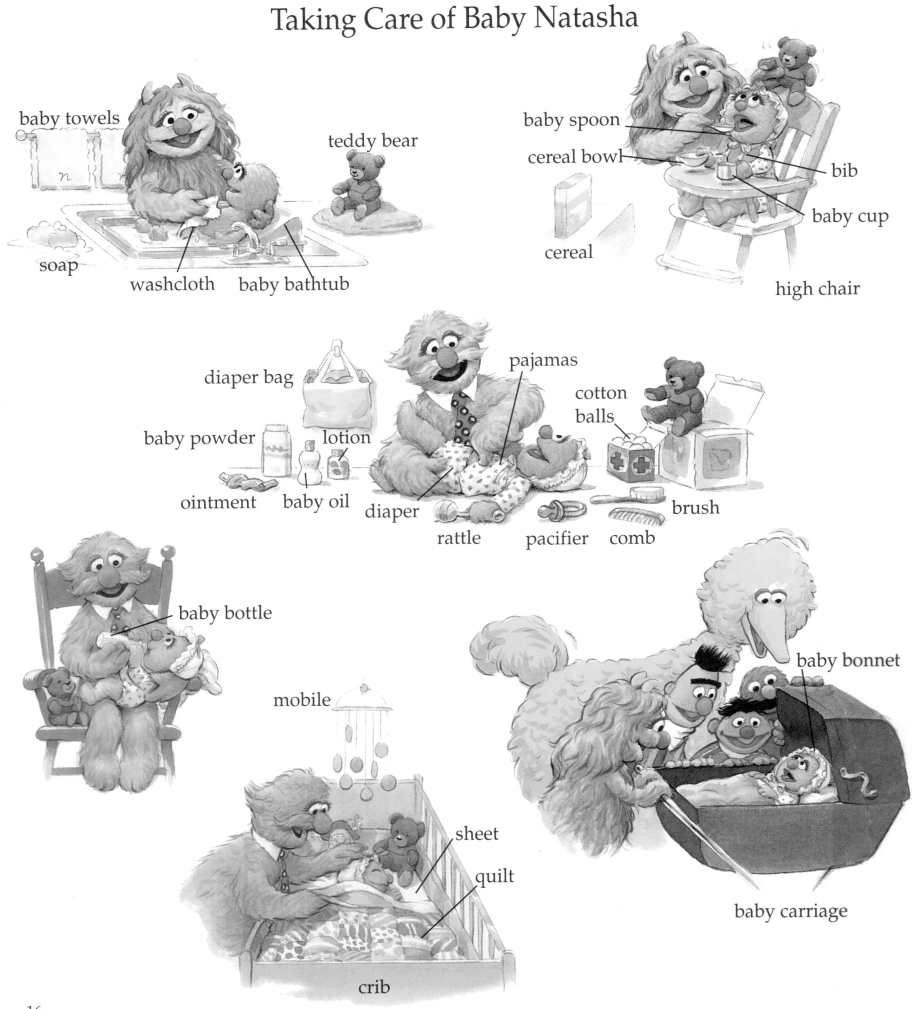

baby towels

teddy bear

soap

washcloth   baby bathtub

baby spoon

cereal bowl

bib

baby cup

cereal

high chair

diaper bag

pajamas

cotton balls

baby powder   lotion

ointment   baby oil   diaper

rattle   pacifier   comb

brush

baby bottle

baby bonnet

mobile

sheet

quilt

crib

baby carriage

16

The Count Counts

1 one Count

2 two bat cars

3 three capes
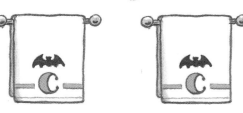

4 four towels

5 five family portraits

6 six bells

7 seven black cats

8 eight mirrors

9 nine spider webs

10 ten toy ships

17

Bert Goes to the Doctor

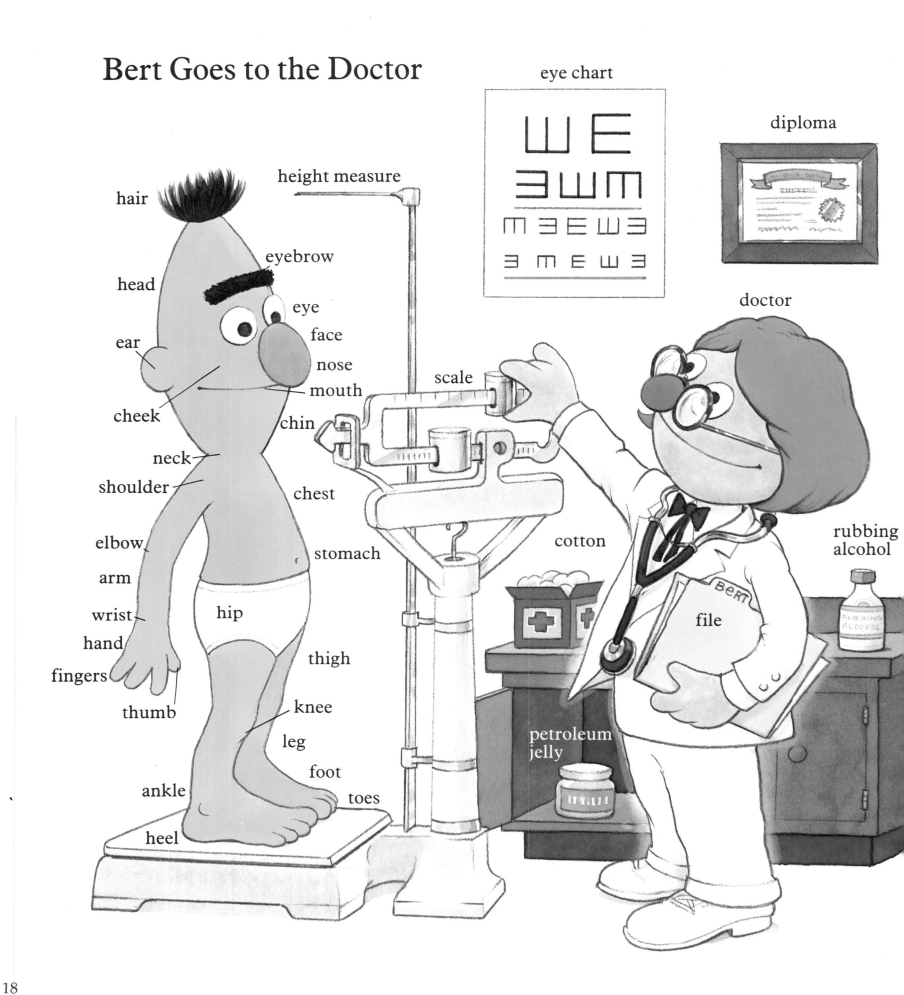

eye chart

diploma

hair

head

ear

cheek

neck

shoulder

elbow

arm

wrist

hand

fingers

thumb

ankle

heel

eyebrow

eye

face

nose

mouth

chin

chest

stomach

hip

thigh

knee

leg

foot

toes

height measure

scale

doctor

cotton

rubbing alcohol

file

petroleum jelly

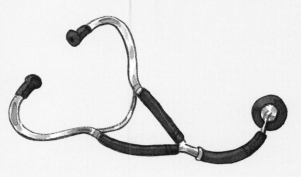
stethoscope

tongue depressor

otoscope

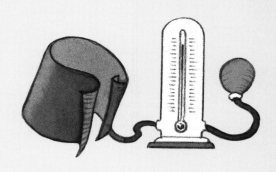
blood-pressure cuff

During Bert's checkup, the doctor . . .

listens to Bert's heart,

looks in Bert's ears

and down his throat,

tests Bert's eyesight,

tests Bert's reflexes,

takes Bert's blood pressure

and temperature,

and gives Bert a shot to help keep him well.

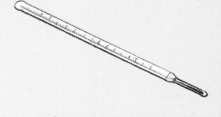

flashlight

reflex hammer

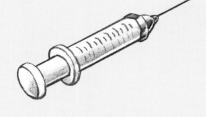
hypodermic needle

thermometer

19

flag

chalkboard

good morning

plant

clock

chalk

easel

teacher

eraser

brushes

chair

globe

apple

desk

student

wastebasket

clay

modeling stick

20

Big Bird at School

Big Bird is painting a picture of one
of his friends. Can you tell who it is?

calendar

bulletin board

alphabet chart

fish tank

record player

sink

table

paper

book

pencil

pen

puzzle

blocks

desk

paper dolls

paper cups

crayon

scissors

paste

paint

Big Bird has stepped
on Herry's toe.
Big Bird is sorry.

Telly has dropped his
backpack into the stream.

Bert has found a rock.
He is excited.

sleeping
bag

rock

toe

pocketknife

canteen

backpack

22

The Great Outdoors

Scout Leader Grover is taking his friends hiking in the woods.

flag

Betty Lou has climbed a hill. She proudly plants her scout flag.

scarf

tree

hill

bee

beehive

Barkley has bumped into a beehive. Now the bees are buzzing!

bush

Grover has found some wildflowers. They are very pretty.

rabbits

Farely crosses the stream very carefully.

Prairie Dawn has discovered a rabbit family. She is surprised!

walking stick

stream

hiking boots

wildflowers

23

Playing in the Park
Bert has brought his pet pigeon Bernice to the park to play with her friends.

jogger

tree

baby carriage

flowers

litter basket

sprinkler

Big Bird hides.

bench

grass

lamppost

pigeons

scooter

Grover falls.

hide-and-seek

skateboard

tricycle

jacks

24

catch

stick ball

barrel

jungle gym

slide

swings

jump rope

bicycle

Herry hops.

hopscotch

Cookie Monster jumps.

Prairie Dawn runs.

sandbox

seesaw

Ernie leaps.

Elmo chases Zoe.

tag

leapfrog

25

Spring

This is the Monster family's back yard.
It is a windy spring day.

chimney

telephone pole

kite

house

garage

fence

car

window box

forsythia

picnic table

shrubs

maple tree

shovel

seeds

stake

hoe

crocus

lawn

robin

lawn mower

dock

nest

toy sailboat

apple tree

ducklings

turtle

duck

mud

pond

daffodils

violets

fern

pussy willows

26

Summer

It's hot. The little Monsters
go swimming to cool off.

lemonade

watermelon

barbecue grill

zinnias

bat

baseball

baseball glove

vegetable garden

underwater mask

water wings

flippers

sunglasses

diver

swimmer

fish

cattails

frog

lily pad

water lily

Autumn

It's cool and the leaves are starting to fall.

geese

pumpkin

rake

cider

corn stalks

leaves

football
helmet

football

soccer ball

apples

acorn

squirrel

28

Winter
It's cold and snowy.
Everyone bundles up.

icicle

toboggan

skis

hat

snow blower

sled

top hat

snowball

snowsuit

broom

parka

boots

snowman

scarf

earmuffs

puck

mittens

snow shovel

ice skates

hockey stick

ice

29

Farmer Grover's Farm
Farmer Grover's friends are
helping him do the chores.

pasture

wheat field

sheep

fence

pickup
truck

hay wagon

lima beans

scarecrow

barrels

well

rake

corn

garden

wheelbarrow

milk can

string beans

carrots

lettuce

tomatoes

hoe

tractor

apple trees

eggs

basket

apples

farmer

henhouse

rooster

30

ladder

hen

baby chicks

chimney

weather vane

farmhouse

pulley

hay bales

barn

silo

hayloft

stalls

hose

dog

pitchfork

goat

bucket

horse

colt

pail

cow

pig

piglets

pigpen

duck

ducklings

duck pond

31

All Over Town

Sherlock Hemlock, the world's greatest detective,
is looking all over town for Barkley the dog.
Can you find Barkley?

hospital

general store

dry cleaner

shoe store

church

cemetery

gas station

restaurant

office building

baker

paw prints

bank

BUS DEPOT

ice-cream parlor

drugstore

barbersho

NATIONAL BANK

BANK

LOADING ZONE

bus

32

rist

hardware store

synagogue

police station

library

school

playground

post office

UNITED STATES POST OFFICE

statue

Town Hall

fire station

bookstore

paw prints

NE COMPANY NO. 177

TOM'S BOOKS

Main Street

33

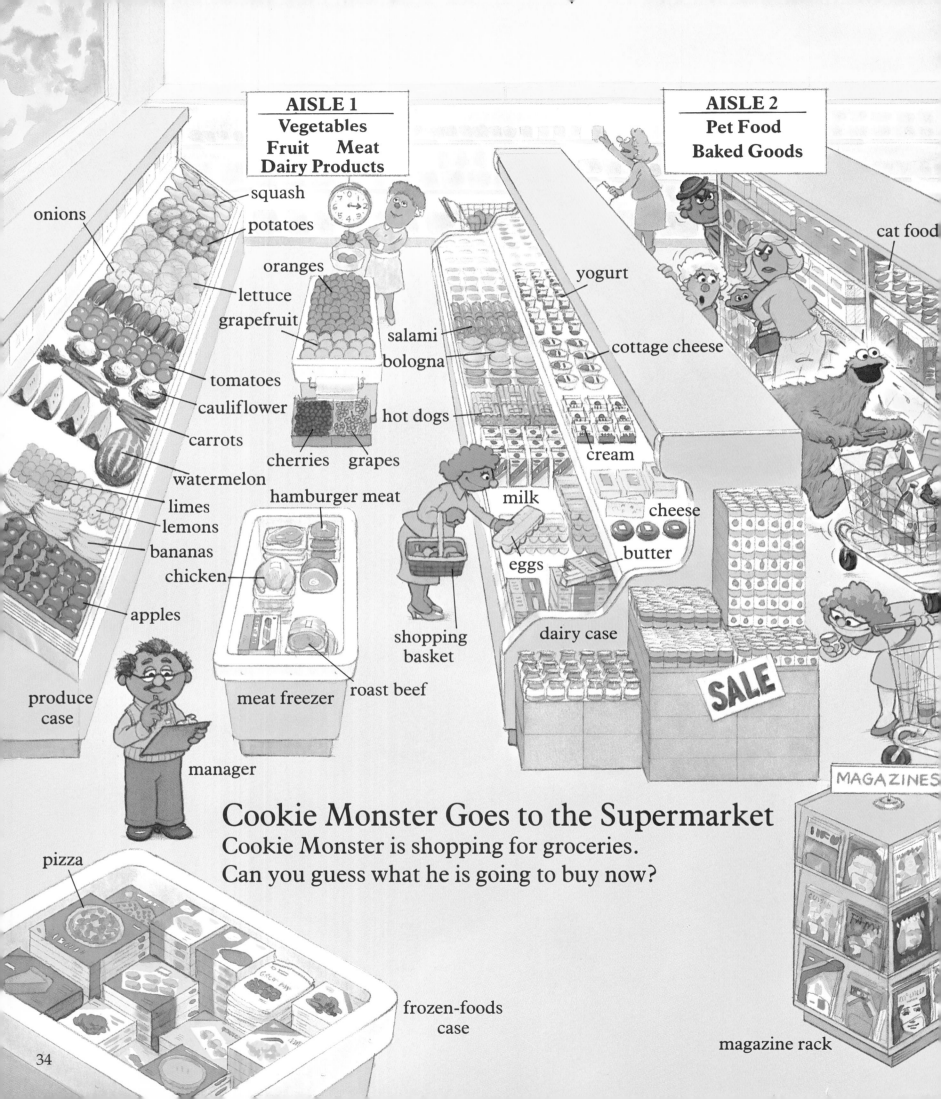

Vegetables
Fruit   Meat
Dairy Products

Pet Food
Baked Goods

squash
onions
potatoes
oranges
lettuce
grapefruit
salami
bologna
tomatoes
cauliflower
hot dogs
carrots
cherries   grapes
watermelon
hamburger meat
limes
lemons
bananas
chicken
apples
cat food
yogurt
cottage cheese
cream
milk
cheese
eggs
butter
shopping basket
dairy case
produce case
meat freezer   roast beef
manager
SALE

Cookie Monster Goes to the Supermarket
Cookie Monster is shopping for groceries.
Can you guess what he is going to buy now?

pizza

MAGAZINES

frozen-foods case

magazine rack

34

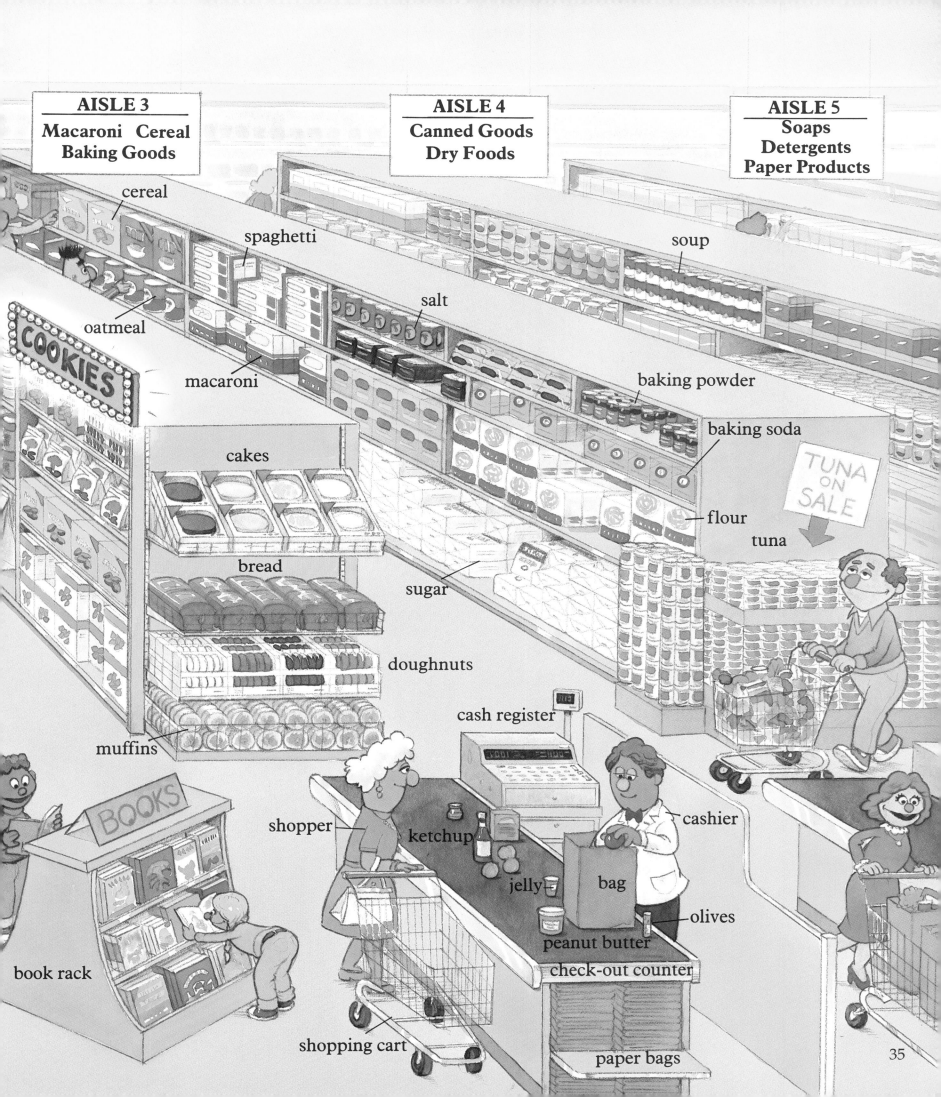

AISLE 3
Macaroni Cereal
Baking Goods

AISLE 4
Canned Goods
Dry Foods

AISLE 5
Soaps
Detergents
Paper Products

cereal

spaghetti

soup

oatmeal

salt

COOKIES

baking powder

macaroni

baking soda

cakes

TUNA
ON
SALE

flour

bread

tuna

sugar

doughnuts

muffins

cash register

BOOKS

shopper

cashier

ketchup

book rack

jelly

bag

olives

peanut butter

check-out counter

shopping cart

paper bags

35

train

moving van

trailer truck

delivery van

school bus

electric car

glazier's truck

ice-cream truck

garbage truck

taxi

car

unicycle

motorcycle

police car

36

Traffic Jam in the City

Here come the fire engines!
Everyone on the street must
pull over to the side to let
the fire trucks through.

pickup
truck

tank truck

pumper truck

hook-and-ladder truck

pushcart

weather instruments

air traffic controller

runway

passenger terminal

control tower

cargo plane

cargo loader

Big Bird at the Airport
Granny Bird is coming to visit. Big Bird is meeting her at the airport.

pilot

propeller plane

cargo

WELCOME GRANNY BIRD!

guardrail

observation deck

38

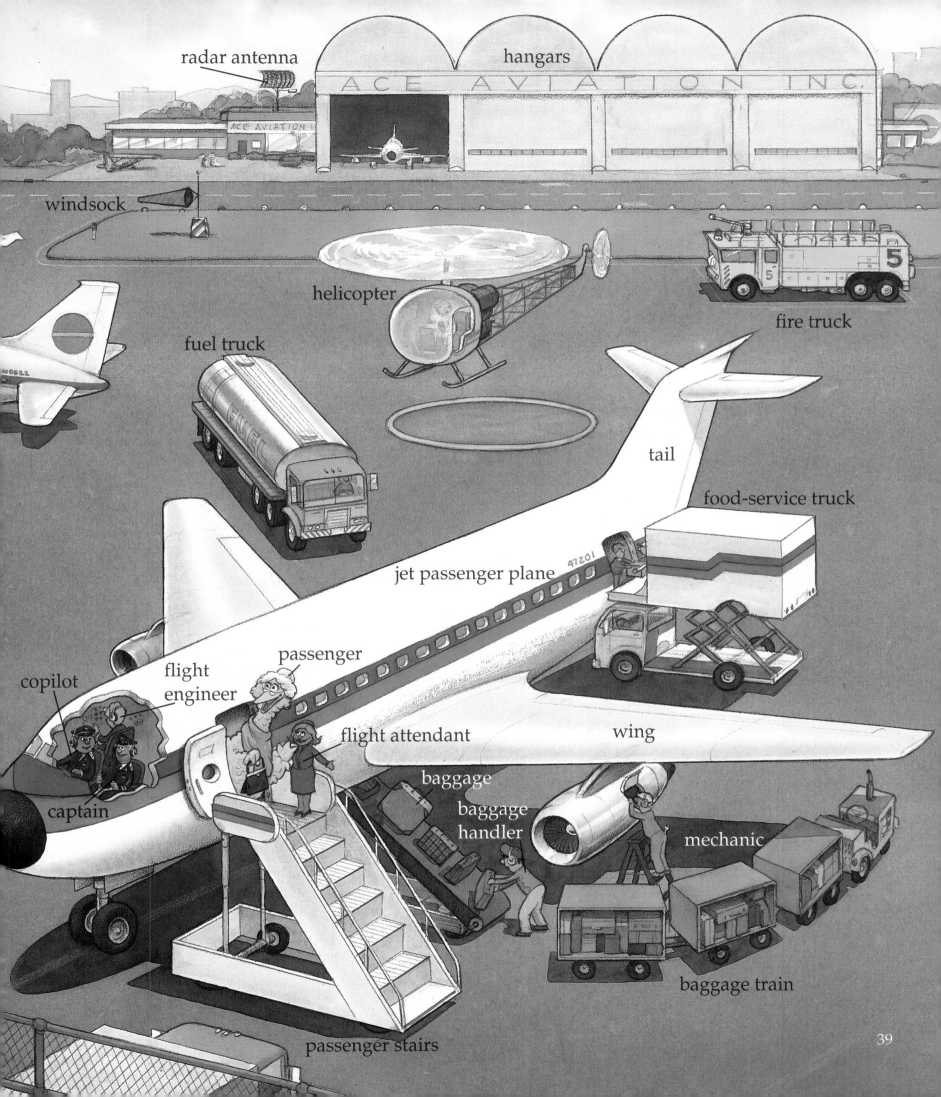

radar antenna

hangars

ACE AVIATION INC.

ACE AVIATION

windsock

fire truck

5

helicopter

fuel truck

FUEL

tail

food-service truck

jet passenger plane

47201

copilot

flight engineer

passenger

flight attendant

wing

captain

baggage

baggage handler

mechanic

passenger stairs

baggage train

39

smokestack

mast

periscope

stern

submarine

ocean liner

bow

motorboat

Coast Guard cutter

seaplane

pontoon

seagulls

tugboat

Captain Oswaldo

houseboat

life preserver

gangwa

CHANNEL FERRY

pier

garbage

GOODBYE

fishing net

barge

dock worker

passenger

fishing trawler

crate

Oscar in the Harbor
Oscar is going on a vacation cruise.
His friends have come to say goodbye.

dock

40

buoy

oil tanker

lighthouse

sailboat

jetty

floating derrick

pilothouse

lifeboat

fireboat

pilings

POLICE

police boat

ferryboat

cargo hoist

forklift truck

cargo

hold

warehouse

container ship

tractor-trailer truck

PIER 6

41

plumb line

Masons

Hod Carrier

pipes

Plumbers

blowtorch

bricks

mason's level

mortar

trowel

scaffolding

Welder

hammer

saw

Carpenters

sawhorse

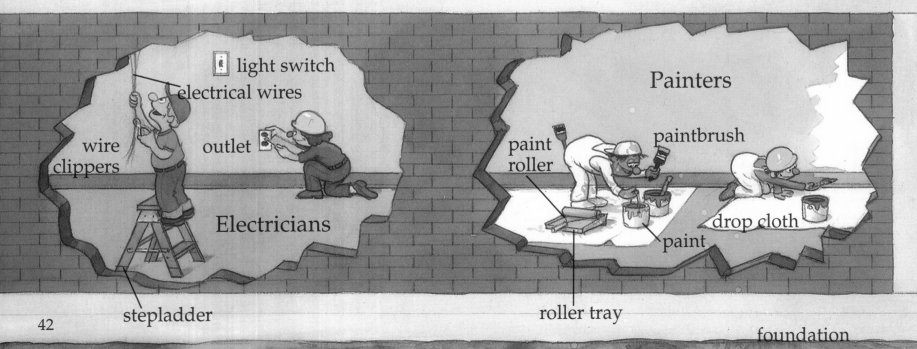

light switch

electrical wires

Painters

wire clippers

outlet

paint roller

paintbrush

Electricians

drop cloth

paint

42

stepladder

roller tray

foundation

girders

Architect

Foreman

blueprints

Construction Site
A new apartment house is under construction on Sesame Street. It takes many workers and many machines to complete the building.

scoop loader

crane

dump truck

power shovel

bulldozer

cement mixer

back hoe

cement

43

The Furry Arms Hotel

There's always room for guests at the Furry Arms Hotel.
Baby Natasha's parents help their visitors check in and check out.

lamp

plant

column

bellhop

suitcase

luggage cart

carpet

purse

44

telephone

key rack

mailboxes

package

letter

key

credit card

teacup

bell

registration book

front desk

45

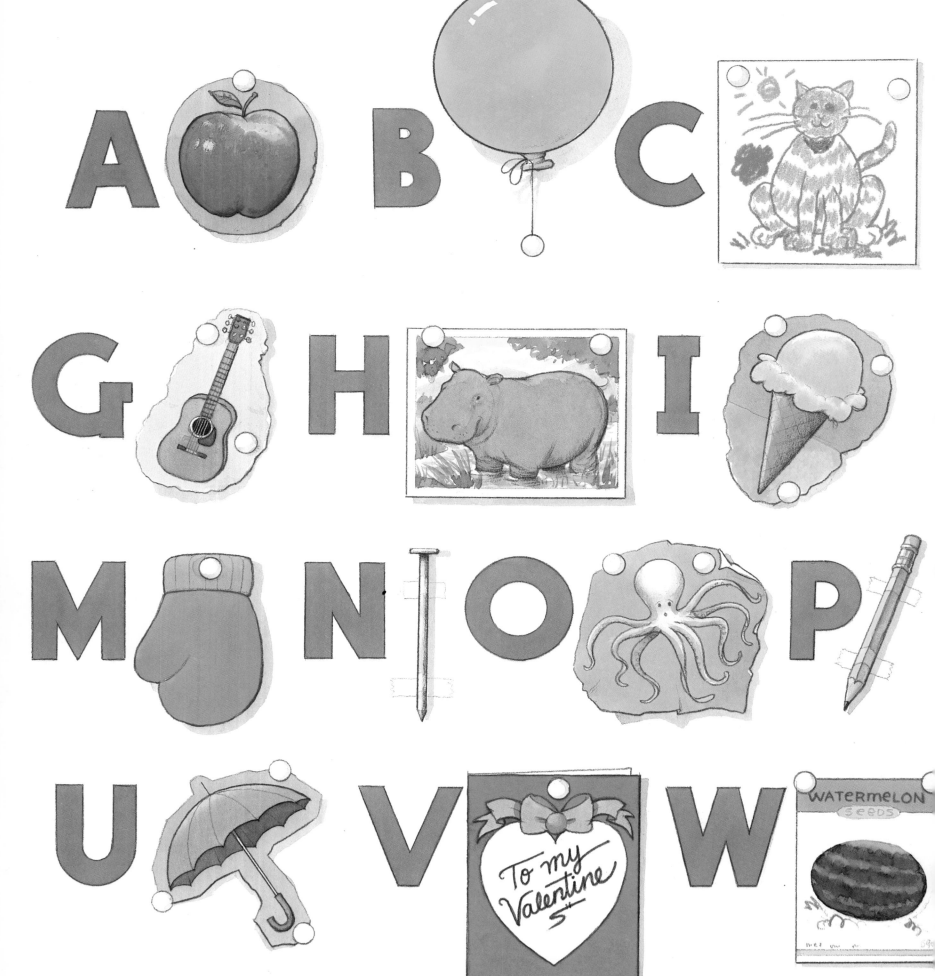